The Car Wash

written by Pam Holden
illustrated by Michael Cashmore-Hingley

For as long as John could remember, his Dad had driven an old blue truck that rattled and bumped along. But one day he proudly drove home in a shiny, new red car. He gave short rides to all his friends and family, then he took John on a long drive to visit Grandpa. The trip took four hours because Grandpa's town was so far away.

For the first hour, Dad and John sang songs together. That was fun, but after an hour, they had sung all the songs they could remember. "How far is it now, Dad?" asked John, looking at the clock near the steering wheel. "We have gone a quarter of the way," Dad answered.

For the second hour, they took turns telling riddles and jokes. Then they played a guessing game called 'I Spy'. After an hour, they were tired of games.
"Are we nearly at Grandpa's town?" John asked.
"We are only halfway there," Dad told him, pointing to the clock.

4

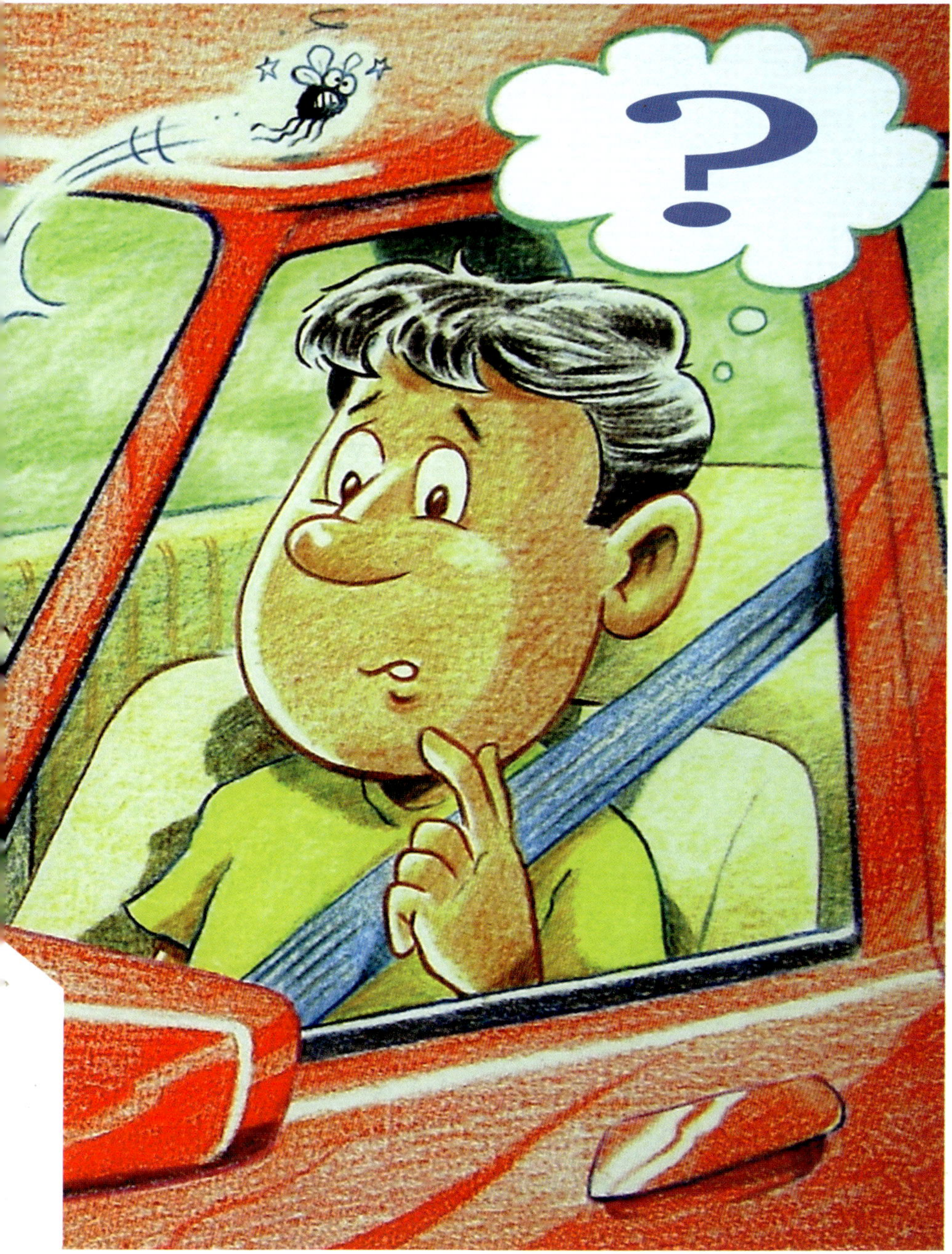

For the third hour, Dad told stories about the lakes, mountains and forests that they were driving past.
"I'm sure we must be getting close now," said John.
"No, there is still another hour to drive," answered Dad.
"We are three-quarters of the way through the trip. Let's play some nice music on the radio."

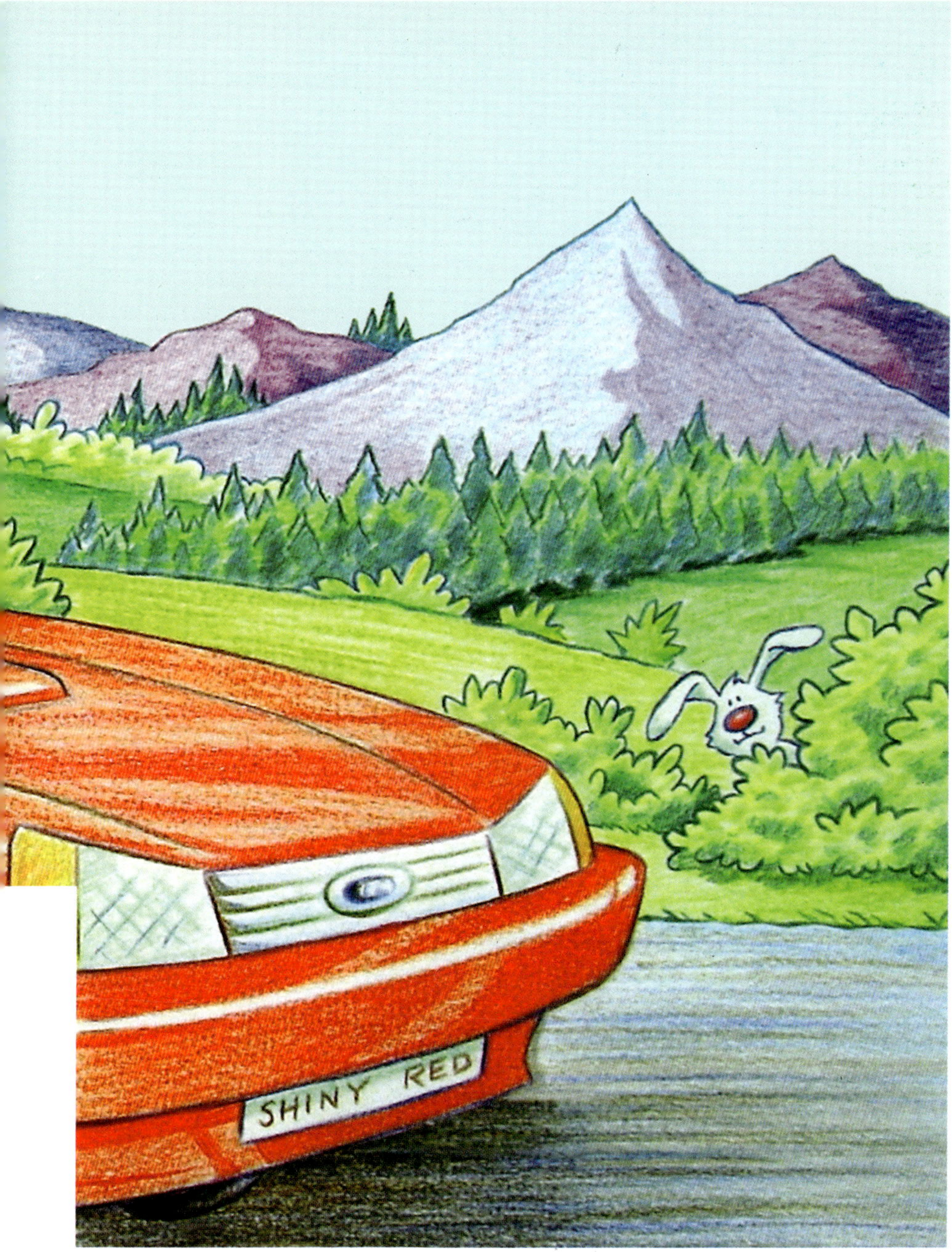
SHINY RED

Before long, John fell asleep. He dreamed about huge giants marching over the mountains, fierce animals in the dark forests, and strange monsters swimming in the lakes. While he slept, Dad drove over muddy roads and through deep puddles. His new car was getting covered with splashes of mud, so Dad decided to go to a car wash before arriving at Grandpa's house.

9

When John woke up, it was as dark as night in the car. At first he thought he must be inside a tunnel or a cave, but outside he saw something frightening. Green jungle vines were slapping against the windows on the left side of the car! Brown branches and leaves were brushing against the windows on the right side! There were strange sounds of swishing and bubbling.

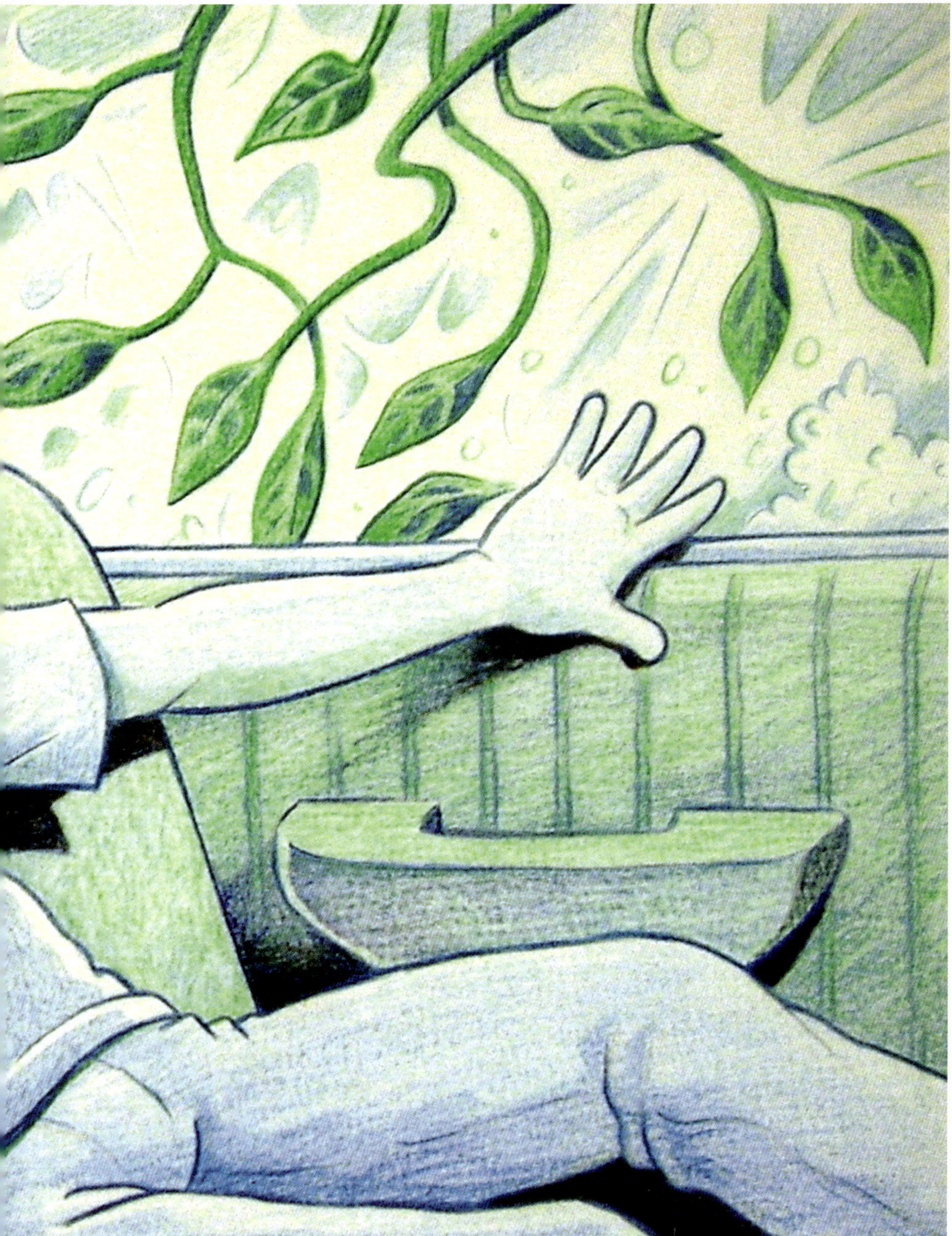

Thick white clouds were covering the front of the car. Water was splashing down the back and side windows like a waterfall or a wave from the sea.

John could see long snakes twisting and slithering by on one side, while huge birds flapped by on the other side. When he felt the car shaking and bumping, he thought of thunderstorms and earthquakes. He remembered learning about dangerous volcanoes and tsunamis.

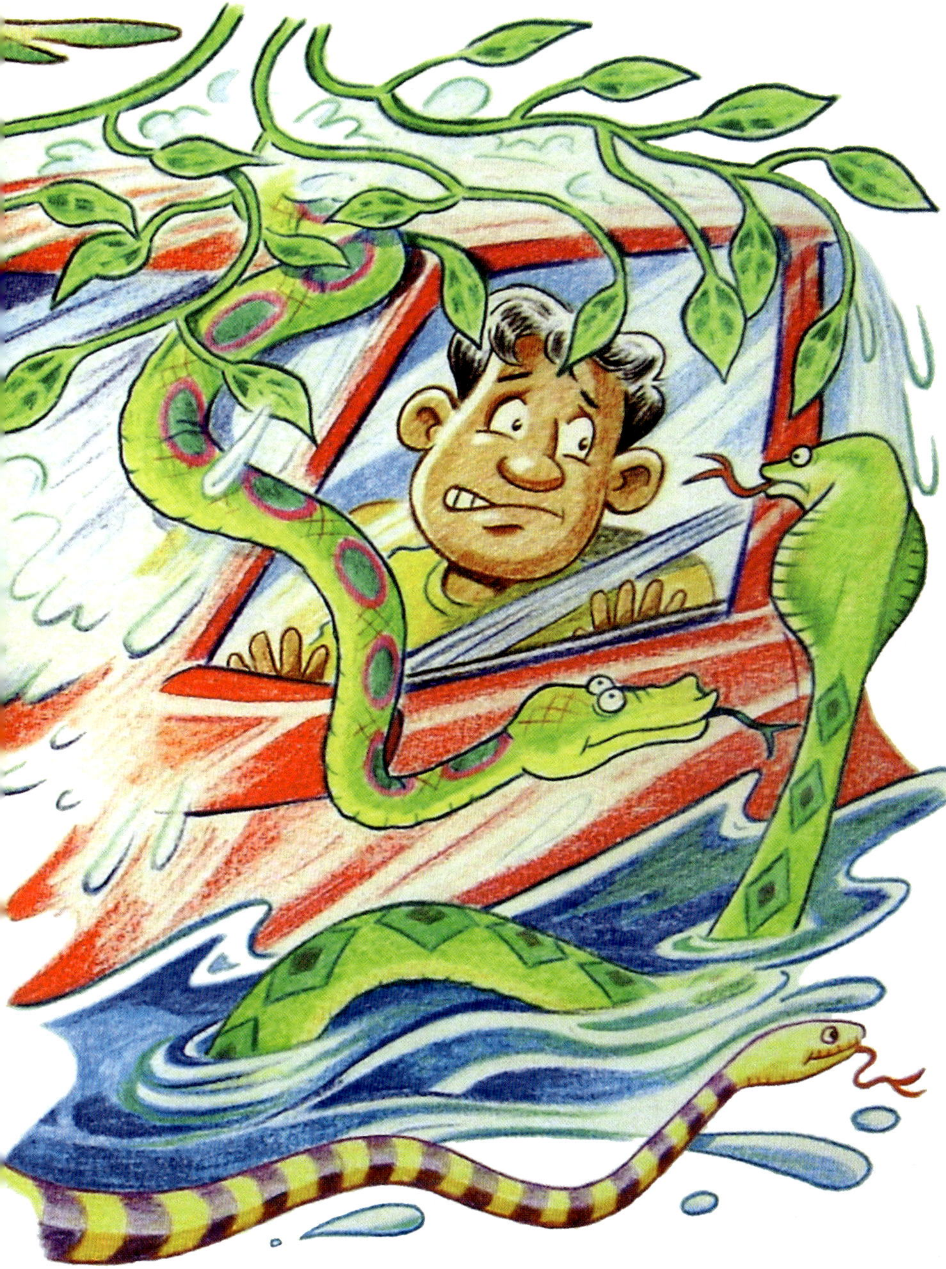

John sat up straight with a loud frightened yell.
"Dad! Help! Where are you? What's happening to us? What's happening outside the car?"
Suddenly the noise and the darkness had gone. In the bright daylight, John could see Dad smiling at him. "You have been asleep for an hour," he said. "You must have been dreaming. The noise of the car wash woke you up. We want our new car to be clean and shiny to visit Grandpa, don't we? Here we are!"

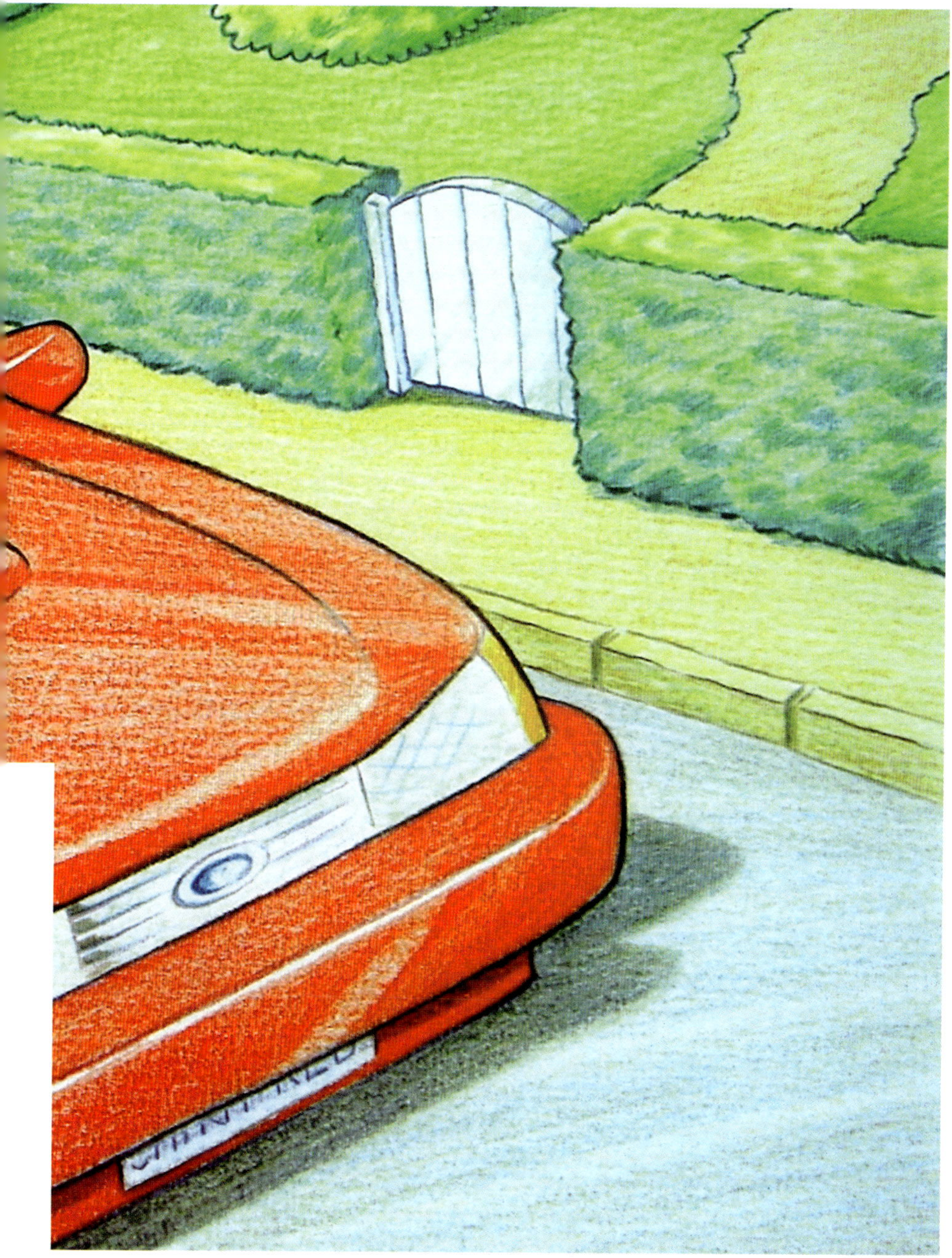

"Welcome!" called Grandpa as he came to meet them.
"I'm pleased to see you both. Did you have a good trip?
I hope it wasn't too tiring or boring, for you, John.
What a bright, shiny car you have!"